THE BIKER'S CAPTIVE
UNDERGROUND CROWS MC BOOK THREE

SADIE KING

LET'S BE BESTIES!

A few times a month I send out an email with new releases, special deals and sneak peeks of what I'm working on. If you want to get on the list I'd love to meet you!

You'll even get a free short and steamy romance when you join.

Sign up here:
www.authorsadieking.com/free

THE BIKER'S CAPTIVE

She was in danger, so I took her...

The moment I set eyes on Willow, my heart stops and my body goes into overdrive. She's mine, and no one else will get even a glimpse of her until she realizes we're meant to be together.

Willow thinks I'm holding her prisoner, but I'm keeping her safe from those that would hurt her. But can I keep her safe from the beast inside of me?

When she parades around my cage all innocence, there's only so much a man like me can be restrained...

The Biker's Captive is an age gap instalove romance featuring an OTT obsessed biker and a curvy, innocent younger woman.

www.authorsadieking.com

1
WILLOW

The first thing I notice is the taste of tarmac grit. I lick my lips, trying to figure out why the hell I've got dirt in my mouth, and taste the metallic tang of blood. That isn't good.

My cheek scrapes against the hard surface of the road as I lift my throbbing head, catching gravel on my skin. The ringing in my ears oscillates up and down, making me feel like I'm underwater. But I'm not underwater. I'm lying on the road, and I've got no idea how I got here.

My nostrils flare with the smell of tarmac and something acrid.

White dust floats from the sky and lands on the road next to me. I stare up at the clear sky, confusion warping my brain. It's too thin to be snow, and this is summertime in southern California. It can't be snowing.

Distorted shouts break through the ringing, and I

turn toward the noise. That's when I see my car. If you can call the twisted heap of metal sprawled on the road a car.

I recognize the light blue paint work and the dream catcher that Mom gave me hanging from the smashed rear view mirror, so it must be mine.

The driver door hangs open, the metal twisted and gaping. The airbag has been deployed, and a dark crimson smear slashes through it.

Whose blood is that?

I touch my forehead and my fingers come away red. Seeing the blood on my fingers sends a surge of panic through me, and pain comes crashing into my consciousness.

I've been in a car accident. A bad one by the looks of my car.

Trying not to panic, I do a mental check through my body. My head is throbbing and there's blood on my lip, but I'm still breathing and nothing hurts too badly. Pushing up on my elbows, I try to stand up. That's when I notice my leg. Pain stabs at my ankle so sharp that my vision blurs. There's blood trickling and pooling at the bottom of my leggings, and the sight of so much blood makes my head feel light. I haul myself into a sitting position and try to piece together what happened.

I was driving to Monterey. I decided to take the Pacific Coast Highway for the views. I remember seeing the ocean for the first time, the indigo blue contrasting with the powder blue of the endless sky. The excitement cutting through the grief of the past few weeks.

As I kept driving, the blue sky turned a burnt shade of orange and then darkened.

I remember yawning as I passed hotels but didn't want to stop and spend money when I was only a few hours out from my destination.

The last thing I remember was the sound of motorbikes on the road. The engines so loud it felt like they were surrounding me.

I remember swiveling in my seat to see why they were so noisy. How I smiled at the sight of a motorcycle gang on the highway, so quintessentially Californian.

There was a black van among the bikes, and I noticed too late how erratically it was driving.

I don't remember what happened next. How I got hit or how I got from the wreck of my car to the middle of the road.

I just know that I'm hurt. I need help, and I need to get off the road.

Something light tumbles toward me on the road. A small rectangular piece of paper. I catch it in my fingers.

It's a $100 bill. And there's more of them, fluttering across the road. I'm wondering what the hell money is doing in the road when there's a shout that pierces through the ringing in my ears.

I look up past my mangled car and for the first time really see the scene in front of me.

The black van is sideways across the road, the front dented and steam gushing from its engine. The side of it is mangled, two ends folding in on themselves, concertinaed together.

A bike lies sprawled on its side, front wheel turning slowly. The engine cuts through the ringing in my ears.

There're at least half a dozen men, their voices panicked and angry. A man crab walks along the ground, snatching the one hundred dollar bills up with his thick hands as white powder floats around him.

I try to call out to him, but my breath catches. Something is wrong with this scene. Very wrong.

There's a man standing in the middle of the road. His arms are outstretched as he looks up at the sky as if asking WTF just happened.

His back is to me, and I can make out the symbol on his jacket: Underground Crows MC.

He stands like a biker, his feet planted solidly on the ground, unfazed by the carnage that surrounds him. Like he welcomes this destruction.

A shiver goes down my spine as I watch him turn around slowly toward me. I'm both curious and terrified to see his face.

The man's smiling, as if he's enjoying all this. And as he turns around, headlights from the upturned bike catch his eyes. Illuminated in the darkness, they look pure black.

The man's eyes lock on mine, and I hold my breath.

He stops in his slow spin, and for a moment we stare at each other. He's got short, cropped hair and the hint of stubble clinging to his solid jaw.

It's not an unpleasant-looking face, and if I wasn't so terrified I might even find him attractive, in a villain enjoying watching the world burn kind of a way.

Someone picks up the bike that's on the ground, and the man's face falls into shadow. But he doesn't stop staring at me.

With his eyes locked on mine, he presses one finger to his pursed lips. I can't hear him, but I know he's telling me to shush.

Indignation rises in my chest. I've just been in an accident that mangled the shit out of my car, and this guy's trying to silence me.

I'm about to call out to the man, but there's something about his look that makes me pause. The smile's gone. His brows are knit together, and he's lost the basking in disaster look. Instead, he looks concerned, almost fearful.

His hands come up in a placating way, and he takes a step towards me as if I'm a wounded animal he has to approach carefully.

There's a shout from behind him, and the man turns away.

My attention snaps to another man rushing to scoop up white bricks that are scattered in the road. And as he picks one up, white powder cascades out of it, catching in the air and blowing on the wind. His face contorts in anger, and he gives a pained wail.

Then it clicks. The white bricks, the money, the powder, the men in their biker cuts.

Oh shit. Oh shit. Oh shit.

It's a drug deal, and I've crashed right in the middle of it.

Since I crawled from my car, everything has been in slow motion, but all of a sudden, it speeds up.

I look for the man trying to shush me, but he's gone. As far as I can tell, he's the only one who noticed me. The other men are too busy scooping up drugs and chasing money across the road.

I need to get out of here before they see me.

Staying close to the ground, I slither across the tarmac, trying to put as much distance between myself and the crash as possible. There's a ditch on the side of the road and beyond that a thicket of bushes. It's not much, but it's my best chance of cover.

Pain courses through my leg when I move but I grit my teeth, forcing myself not to cry out.

I'm almost at the edge of the road when a yell goes up behind me. Turning, my gaze snaps to the source.

A short, stocky man with big, angry eyebrows faces me from the other side of the road. He wears a biker's jacket, but the patch is different from the other man's.

He looks straight at me and his lips curl, barring his teeth. He takes a step toward me, pulling a gun from his hip.

A shock of terror jolts my body.

The wreck of my car lies between us and he's holding his side as if he's injured, but I still know it won't take him long to reach me.

I've witnessed something here that I shouldn't have. I know how things like this work. They can't have any witnesses.

I pull myself up, ignoring the throbbing pain in my leg.

Run, Willow. Run.

I take a step forward and my leg gives way underneath me, sending me crashing to the ground. I hit the tarmac and feel the jolt through my whole body.

When I look up, the man is staggering toward me. He's holding his side, his lips curled up in a grimace. If he wasn't so injured, he'd be over here by now.

But his injuries give me the chance I need to escape.

Come on, come on.

I pull myself up onto my elbows and then up to my knees.

My vision goes blurry with pain, but I need to move. I need to move now.

If I reach the thicket, maybe I can hide out and get away from these men.

Excruciating pain shoots through my leg, but somehow I manage to drag myself to the side of the road.

I risk a glance over my shoulder, and the man is now halfway across the road. He's stumbling as much as I am, which is the only reason why I'm still alive.

The white line blurs in front of me, and I'm not sure if it's the head injury or the pain making me lightheaded.

If I lose consciousness now, I'll never wake up.

The rev of a bike engine close by startles me, making me scream in terror. I spin around, expecting to find a gun pointed at me.

But it's not the man with the gun. It's the other one. The giant who tried to shush me. He straddles his bike with one leg cocked and indicates the seat behind him.

"Get on."

I stare at the man on the bike, scanning his face for something soft, something gentle, but he's deadpan and he gives nothing away, just those intense eyes staring at me.

"Get on now."

It's the urgency in his voice that makes me move. I take a step toward him and stumble forward. In an instant he slides off his bike and catches me under my shoulders.

I'm half dragged, half stumble toward his bike. I cry out as my sore leg bumps against him. Then he's lifting me up, pulling my limp body onto his bike.

My face scratches against his stubble, and I smell blood and the ocean. Then he spins me around, nestling my body in front of him.

The bike moves beneath me, and I grab hold of the handlebars to stop from sliding off. A gunshot rings out behind us and the man swerves from side to side, each swerve sending new pain through my body.

He steers the bike through the wreckage, away from the gunshots, and soon we leave the carnage behind.

I don't know why he did it. I don't know why he saved me. But as the bike vibrates gently beneath me, I slump against the man and lose consciousness.

2
PANS

A bullet hits the tarmac by my feet, and I gun the accelerator. My bike swerves around the carnage as another shot's fired.

I lean forward, shielding the woman's body as we speed down the highway. She moans softly and her body slumps, unconscious. I tighten my thighs around hers and tense my arms, holding her in place.

The shouts behind us become more distant as we leave the scene behind, but I don't let myself relax yet.

I don't know what state the other bikes are in, but if anyone from The Reapers follows us, I know exactly what they'll do. Whoever this woman is, she witnessed something she shouldn't have. The quicker I can get her to safety, the better.

I hazard a glance behind us, but there are no telltale headlights following. I take the next off ramp just in case, knowing I can lose them in the winding clifftop roads that surround this area.

I know every inch of these roads and every tilt my bike needs to make, but I take the corners slower than usual with my precious cargo leaning on me the whole time.

When I saw this beauty sprawled in the road, her foot twisted and a blood spot on her cheek, I knew instantly I'd do whatever it takes to protect her.

I saw the moment she realized what she was caught in the middle of. I saw the realization on her face and then the terror.

She's a civilian caught between two gangs. It's been a long time since I left the military, but I still have an urge to protect civilians, especially pretty, curvy ones.

As we climb further into the hills, we leave the freeway far behind, and I'm confident now that no one is following us.

I left four of my brothers at the wreck, but they were all on their feet and in one piece. The Pres would want me to protect a woman. The other guys can deal with The Reapers.

Twenty minutes later, I've got a dead arm as we pull onto the gravel road that leads to the cottage. Dense trees surround this private road, and the nearest neighbors are miles away.

It's the club cottage, not my own, and the location is a well-guarded secret. There's no way The Reapers will find her here.

We pull up to the cottage, and I kill the engine. The noise of the woods closes in, insects chirping in the night, the rustling of leaves from the wind, and the distant sound of waves crashing against the cliffs.

It's peaceful up here. My escape, and also where I do my best work for the club.

The woman groans softly as I lift her off the bike. Blood trickles down her leg, but she's still breathing. She's also still unconscious, and I hoist her over my shoulder so I can unlock the door and get us inside.

I carry her straight down to the basement. If anyone did follow me here, it's best to keep her where she won't be seen.

There's a thin mattress on a bench, and this is where I lay her down. She doesn't stir, and I take a moment to sit back and look at her properly.

My breath catches in my throat.

The brief glimpse I got of her in the headlights showed she was a beauty, but down here in the full light, I can see how stunning she is.

The woman's hair hangs in a thick golden rope which I pull over her shoulder. Tendrils have escaped the plait, falling around her temples and framing her plump, pale lips and impossibly smooth skin.

She's got to be almost twenty years younger than me, which makes the stirring in my pants slightly wicked, but I've never claimed to be a saint.

She's wearing a thin cotton dress over leggings. And

God help me, I can't help staring at her plump breasts pressed up against the flimsy fabric, the outline of a white lacy bra showing through the thin cotton.

My dick stirs, and my blood heats.

A protective energy runs through me so sudden and powerful that I grip the sides of the bench.

One word forms on my lips.

Mine.

This woman is mine, and I won't let any of my brothers see her.

I saw her, I rescued her, and I'll keep her here away from prying eyes until she's healed.

She moans softly, her lips parting in a groin-tingling pout. She looks so innocent, so vulnerable. A trickle of blood runs down her bottom lip, and I'm jolted back to reality.

This is no time to get off on her perfect plump body. This woman needs medical attention. She needs my help.

I know my way around the human body. I wish I could say it was from the military. But the things I'm tasked to do for my MC brothers have given me a good understanding of how a human is put together. Exactly how deep you can cut and where to cause maximum pain but not bleed out. I'm usually pulling people apart, not putting them back together. But the principles are the same.

A quick scan tells me her wounds are surface level, but that won't make them hurt any less.

I pull over my cabinet of instruments. I skip the top drawer, because I won't be needing those today, and pull open the second drawer.

There's a bottle of alcohol and a dirty bandage. I'm usually not worried if my subject gets infected. But tonight is different. I need to clean her wounds and disinfect them.

My eyes cast to her cotton dress. It needs to come off anyway to check her over, and it's quicker than going upstairs to grab a dishcloth.

My hands cross the top of the dress and I pull. The fabric comes away with a satisfying tear.

And God help me, my dick hardens.

This girl's lying there with blood on her and injuries, but the animal inside of me can't stop wondering what she'd look like with my dick in her mouth.

"Focus," I mutter to myself.

Drawing my eyes away from her bare flesh, I tear the dress into cotton strips. Then I pour the alcohol on and use it to clean her wounds.

She's got on a pair of leggings, and I pull those down to check her leg injury.

I can't give myself any good reason to yank her panties off, so they stay on for now. My mouth goes dry as I look at the white cotton panties edged with lace. The delicate fabric circling her soft thighs.

I force myself to focus on her leg.

Blood oozes from a gash above her ankle. A shard of

glass sticks out of her skin that must have gotten lodged in the accident.

In one quick move, I pull the glass out. She cries out, and her eyelids flicker open. She looks at me with drowsy eyes and then falls back asleep. Pulled back to unconsciousness.

Carefully, I clean the wound and wrap a strip of cotton tight around it to stop the bleeding. The ankle is twisted, already starting to turn an angry purple.

The blood on her face looks like it's coming from a graze on her cheek, and it looks worse than it is.

I pop upstairs for some hot water and a flannel and I wash her gently, wiping away the grit and stains from the road.

Slowly I work myself up her body, pressing and prodding as I look for internal injuries. If she's bleeding inside, she'll need more assistance than I can give. But taking her to a hospital right now would be tantamount to murder. The Reapers have people everywhere, and they'll be on the lookout for a young woman with injuries from a car accident.

But she's lucky. The car was totaled, and by some miracle this woman is barely injured.

I gently run my fingers across her cheek, resting my hand on her warm skin. Her hot breath caresses my thumb, and her vulnerability in this moment makes my chest tighten. She looks so vulnerable, so precious.

She's alive, this precious human, and in my care. I

won't let her down. But I need to check that she'll wake up again.

"Precious," I whisper.

There's nothing, so I say it again a bit louder. "Wake up, precious."

Her eyes flutter open. They're as blue as the summer skies of California. Her eyes meet mine. And she gives me half a smile before she passes out again.

I can't leave her like this with nothing on, and I've ripped her dress to shreds. I keep a bag of clothes here. I go upstairs and grab one of my old t shirts.

When I bring it downstairs, she's still sleeping in just her bra and panties.

Sometimes there's a darkness inside of me that rises up like a beast. It's a part of me, part of who I am. And sometimes I let the beast out and I let the darkness erupt inside of me as I do terrible things.

I feel that beast stir inside me now.

I'm overcome with the urge to rip her white cotton panties off to see exactly how her pussy looks underneath.

My trembling hands go to the edge of the panties. I slip my fingers under the lace trim.

The elastic feels tight, a soft pressure on my fingers. I can feel the tip of her course thick hair against my fingertips.

My breathing comes hard and fast. The beast in me wanting to rip her panties off and do dark things.

Then I look at her innocent face, her clear, blemish-free skin. Her full innocent lips. And I remind myself who I am. I rescued this woman, and I'm her protector.

Even if that means protecting her from myself.

Lifting her up with one arm, I slide the t-shirt over her head. It's so big that it covers her straining bra and her cotton panties.

I have kept the beast in check, but for how long?

3
WILLOW

My eyes flicker open, and a fluorescent light swims into my vision. I stare at it for a moment, thoroughly confused about where I am and why.

Then images of the day before swim into my brain. Slowly at first: cruising down the Pacific Coast Highway with George Ezra blaring through the speakers. The sky an impossible orange sunset. Feeling tired but pushing on, needing to get to Mom.

I remember the sound of motorbikes, then the black van that sped past me.

The images come faster now. Crawling on the road, powder in the air, one hundred dollar bills billowing across the tarmac. The smell of burnt metal and the taste of blood. The man who pulled a gun on me and the man who saved me.

I sit up with a start, gasping for breath as the weight of what happened settles on my chest.

A warm hand clasps mine and it's my rescuer, disheveled and unshaven, dark circles under his eyes.

His hand squeezes mine, and it's the reassurance of his touch that calms my racing heart.

We stare at each other, and his gaze is no less intense under the fluorescent lights than it was amid the carnage of the accident.

"You're safe," he says in a gravelly voice that scrapes over my rough nerves, both calming me and making my spine tingle all at once.

The hand he clasps me with is pocked with red angry scars, the skin puckered and dead, and I wonder what pain he's been through to cause those burns. Up close, I notice the silver flecks peppered through his dark hair and the deep lines etched into his face.

He looks like a man who's seen some shit.

"You're safe with me," he says again as if reading my mind.

Memories swim into my brain of being lifted onto his bike, carried into this place. Swimming in and out of consciousness as this man bathed my sweaty forehead and tended my injuries, his touch impossibly gentle for someone who looks so hard.

"What's your name?" he asks.

I take a few deep breaths, collecting my thoughts. There's something hard about this man, but a gentleness too. I immediately feel I can trust him, and besides, what other options do I have?

"Willow."

"Willow." His deep voice adds a gravelly rumble that belies the wistfulness of my name. I like the way he says it, and it sends a shudder all the way through my body which makes me wince with pain.

"Are you hurting?" His brow furrows with concern.

Hurting doesn't even begin to cover it. I'm confused and in pain and my mouth is dry.

"Yes," I croak. "My leg hurts like a motherfucker."

He smiles at my cuss word, and I'm annoyed at how pleased it makes me to get a reaction out of him.

"I'm Pans."

"Pans. What kind of a name is that?" It slips out before I can stop myself. "Sorry, it's just unusual. I don't mean to be rude."

"It's my road name," he says without explanation. My gaze goes to the leather jacket he's wearing and the MC club insignia there. I have so many questions, but my brain feels hazy.

"You've been in a car accident." That gentle rumble is doing weird things to my body, and I will him to keep talking.

"Where do you live?"

My brain feels muddled from whatever painkillers he must've given me, but even I know you don't give a strange man your address. Even if I did have one.

"It's none of your business."

His hand grips mine. I don't know if he means to be threatening, but all it does is send another shiver through my body.

"Do you have anything in the car, any ID with your address on it?"

I had my driver's license in my purse. But that was the address that I left behind in Seattle. The only address I had was a scribbled note of the place where I could find my mom.

I shake my head, wondering what the hell my address has to do with anything.

"Why do you want to know?"

The man takes a slow breath like he's weighing how much to tell me.

"How much do you remember of the accident?"

I squeeze my eyes tight as images thrash through my head. The pain, the shouting, the blood. A whimper escapes my lips, and the man caresses my arm soothingly.

"Not much."

"The crash you had was with some bad men."

I give him a raised eyebrow look. With his blood-stained t-shirt and biker's jacket, he's what I'd call the definition of a bad man.

He must see me looking at the emblem on his jacket, because he glances down and shakes his head slowly.

"Not us, precious. We're the good guys."

An involuntary snort escapes my nose. His grim look,

the blood, the drugs. There's no way this man's on the right side of the law.

"Really?"

"Trust me," he says. "This is nothing compared to what The Reapers would do to you."

The name sends a shiver down my spine, and this one isn't pleasant.

"The Underground Crows don't run drugs, but it's The Reapers that you crashed into, and it's them I'm worried about."

"What do you mean?"

He tucks a strand of hair behind my ear.

"You'll be safe here, precious. What I need to know is if there's anybody else we need to bring in for protection. Like your family who could be easily traced back to your address."

Bring in for protection. I hear his words, but they don't make sense. The full weight of my situation hits me. I've witnessed some kind of drug run gone wrong and The Reapers, whoever they are, will do anything to silence me, including killing me and those I love.

I've never felt so happy to be an orphan.

I bark out a laugh, and Pans looks confused. But the irony of the situation isn't lost on me. Everyone I love could be in danger, if there was someone still alive I loved.

"You don't have to worry about that," I say. "There's no one else you need to protect."

I can't hide the bitterness from my voice or the sting of tears that threaten. I blink quickly and look away.

Pans gives me a curious look, but he doesn't press.

My answer must satisfy him, because he presses me gently back onto the bed.

"You need to rest, precious." I can't say I mind the pet name he's given me, especially said in his badass voice.

"I need to make a phone call, and I'll be back. You've got food here, everything you need. But don't move too much. I'll come and change the bandages soon."

I'm suddenly aware of the questions I haven't asked, like where the fuck am I?

For the first time, I look around properly at my surroundings. The floor is concrete, and the bed I'm on is nothing more than a low bench with a thin mattress. My dress lies in tatters on the top of a metal cabinet with steel medical instruments laid out on top.

But I'm pretty sure this isn't a medical center.

"Where am I?"

Pan shifts uncomfortably and gets up off the chair he's been sitting on.

"Rest," he says as he turns his back on me.

That's when I notice the metal bars. I don't know how I missed them before. They're by the side of my bench-bed, and they reach all the way up to the ceiling.

"What the fuck?"

I sit up fully, ignoring the pain that throbs in my ankle. But I have to figure this out. The bars go all around me like a cage. I'm in a fucking cage.

As the realization sets in, Pans opens a metal door and steps out of my cell. Because, yeah, that's what the fuck this is.

"Why am I in a cage?" I can't hide the panic in my voice. I've been having a nice teté-a-teté with my rescuer thinking I'm safe only to realize I'm locked up.

He turns to me, and there's real regret in his eyes.

"Sorry, precious. It's for your own protection. It's the safest place for you."

He shuts the metal door with a dull clanging noise and clicks the lock into place.

Fear pools in the pit of my stomach. I'm being held captive by a biker whose touch makes my body tingle.

What the fuck have I gotten myself into?

4

PANS

"*H*ey, come back here."

There's panic in her voice, and I hate that I keep walking up the stairs, but I do. It's for her own protection.

I don't know Willow. I don't know if she'll leave if I don't lock her up. But I have to make sure she doesn't so that The Reapers can't track her down.

I already know if anything happened to her, I'd lose my mind.

She rattles the metal bars, and I force myself to keep looking ahead. Leaving an injured girl locked in the cage is not my best moment. But that's what I need to do to protect her.

I leave the door of the basement ajar, and I can still hear her calling to me as I speed dial Bruno, the club Pres.

We spoke last night and had a debrief about what the fuck happened.

The Reapers have been warned not to bring drugs through our territory. We got a tip-off about a drug run coming straight through our turf. That's not cool with us.

We didn't know the size of the drop when we intercepted them. We expected a few men on bikes, not a van full of heroin. And we didn't expect the driver to be a crazy-ass bastard.

Willow got caught in the middle of it with her car. He swerved right into her, not giving a shit if he hurt anyone else.

The thought makes my fists clench. When I find the asshole who was driving, I'll make him pay for what he did to her. How she survived, how she walked away from that crash, fuck only knows.

She could have fucking died.

The fact that I found Willow, damaged and in need of my help, sends a new wave of protectiveness through me. I long ago stopped believing in a God, but maybe there is fate at work. Maybe something bigger than me has thrown this woman quite literally into my path.

I can't explain the warm feeling I got when her body pressed against mine, holding her between my legs on the bike. And it's not the usual heat of a woman's body. I've had plenty of that, but never have I felt this tightness in my chest as I watch her sleep. When I look at her angelic face, I know I'd kill for her ten times over.

"We've brought the car in, and it's destroyed," says

Bruno, confirming what I already suspected. Willow isn't getting her car back. "We cleared up the wreck before anyone saw. As far as highway patrol knows, there was no crash last night."

I uncurl my fists with relief. No one else will be looking for Willow. There will be no record of the crash. No way for The Reapers to trace her.

Don't get me wrong. If she needed emergency care, I would take her to a hospital. But her wounds are only surface level. I can give her all the care she needs right here.

We know The Reapers won't come for us. They're not stupid enough to start a gang war. But they'll come for a witness if we don't protect her.

"How's the girl?" Bruno asks.

I gave him a rundown of Willow's injuries last night so he knows what I'm dealing with.

"She's going to be fine," I tell him.

"I'm gonna send Gage and Lyle out there to look after her. You can come back and deal with the Reapers."

"No."

It's not often I contradict the Pres, but there's no way in hell I'm letting another man come out here and tend to Willow.

Willow is mine. Mine to look after, mine to protect. Not even my MC brothers are going to get close to her until I know her heart is securely entwined with mine.

"Pans, I'm not sure nursing a witness is the right job

for you," Bruno says carefully. "We want her alive, and we want her to feel safe."

If I was any other man, I might be offended, But I know why Bruno's skeptical. I'm usually pulling people apart, not putting them together.

"Don't worry, Pres. I'll protect this woman with my life."

Bruno goes silent. I'm many dark things, but I'm also a man of my word.

"All right Pans. If you want to play nurse, you do it. But I'm sending Gina to help. This girl needs reassurance. She needs to know she can trust us. I want her to feel safe, not be scared of us."

Again, I'm not offended. I'm not known for making people feel safe and reassured.

Gina's our club manager and resident matriarch. She's no one's old lady; she gave that up a long time ago. But she looks after us and has a knack for putting people at ease with her good nature. I've never met anyone who didn't like Gina.

"Fine," I say. "Send Gina, but no other man gets near Willow."

Bruno chuckles like he can see right through me. But I don't give a shit. If this is what it means to fall in love, then sign me up.

5

WILLOW

*I*t feels like hours since Pans left me alone, but it's hard to tell the time in this place with no windows. My body is weak, and despite the revelation that I'm locked up, I drift into a fitful sleep.

When I wake up, the first thing I see is the solid metal bars, and anger flares up in me.

Clenching my teeth against the pain, I swing my legs over the side of the bench. My feet hit the concrete floor, and I let out a hiss as pain jolts my leg.

I take a few deep breaths, assessing my body and where the pain points are. My ankle appears to be twisted as well as cut, and it hurts to put pressure on it.

But pain I can handle. What I can't handle is being locked up in a fucking cage.

I push myself off the bed and hobble across to the metal door.

Every step is an effort, and sweat pools on my forehead. My body is still weak and I probably shouldn't be out of bed, but fuck that. I shouldn't be in a cage either.

I'm trying to align the man who rescued me and gently tended to my wounds with the man who would lock me in a cage. One action so caring, the other so...weird.

My hands grasp the metal of the door and I pull, but it doesn't give. I don't know what I was expecting. I saw him lock it.

I walk a circle of the cage checking out my surroundings. It's a square metal frame, reaching from the concrete floor to the ceiling above. There's a dark stain on the ground, and I shudder wondering about what has happened in here.

In one corner a low table has a plate of food, and I fall on it eagerly.

The bread of the sandwich is stale and the chicken filling slimy, but I'm too hungry to care. There's a can of soda, and I drink it down in a couple of gulps.

My excursion has made me tired, and I drag myself back to the makeshift bed.

There's a metal trolley next to the bed with strips of my torn dress that Pans used for bandages. Next to the fabric strips is a pair of small scissors, and I slide them into the side of my underwear. Feeling better for having a weapon, even a small one, I collapse exhausted onto the bed.

The scissors dig into my side, and I adjust them so

they're flush against my hip and hidden in my underwear.

I'm wearing an oversized t-shirt that must be Pans's. A thought comes unbidden into my mind of Pans's hands on me as he peeled off my clothes.

I wonder what he thought of my body. I wonder if he liked what he saw. Heat flushes my cheeks, and confusion floods my brain. The man locked me up. I shouldn't be thinking wicked thoughts about him.

Yet there's something about the brooding, troubled biker that makes my skin heat and my insides go all gooey.

There's the sound of the basement door opening and voices on the stairs. I recognize Pans's heavy tread alongside a lighter one.

A woman gasps.

"What the fuck?"

She rushes down the remaining steps, and I sit up on my elbows as she reaches the cage.

"What the fuck, Pans?"

The woman looks to be in her early thirties with her hair scraped back into a ponytail. She's wearing a small denim skirt and a tight black t-shirt, unafraid to show off her substantial body. Under one arm she carries a canvas bag, and I'm pleased there's a fresh loaf of bread poking out the top of it. I like her immediately.

The fact that she's indignant on my behalf also helps.

The woman pulls at the door, and when it doesn't budge, she looks at Pans in disbelief.

"Why's she locked up?"

Pans shrugs, and at least has the decency to look ashamed. "It's for her own protection," he mumbles.

But the woman isn't buying it. Pans opens the latch, and she pushes past him to get in.

She dumps her bag next to me and takes my hand in her plump one.

"I'm sorry he's got you locked up in here, sweetheart. I'm Gina."

The concerned look on her face and the way she's apologizing on Pans's behalf gives me reassurance that at least someone else thinks this whole situation is fucked up.

"It's for her protection." But it sounds like he's trying to convince himself.

Gina gives him a stare that makes the hard-ass Pans look away chastised. She purses her lips together and turns her attention back to me.

"I'm going to change your dressings; I've got proper bandages and I brought fresh food and magazines."

"I'll change the dressings." Pans steps protectively to my side, practically nudging Gina out of the way.

She raises her eyebrows at him, as confused as I am.

"Fine, you do the top half, but this sprained ankle needs attention."

Gina asks me a few questions about myself and the accident while Pans stays silent. I'm tired from my excursion and after a while I lie back and close my eyes, letting them fuss over me.

Pans is at the top end, undoing the bandage around my head. His fingertips brush my temples, and I feel the heat of his breath on my cheek as he leans over to inspect the wound. A delicious shiver goes down my spine, and my eyes flutter open.

He's leaning over me, so close I notice the amber flecks in his deep brown eyes that I missed the other night.

"How's it looking?" I ask.

His gaze flicks to mine, and a bolt of heat shoots straight between my legs. I clench my thighs, hoping that no one notices. It's disconcerting that the man holding me captive also makes my body do things I can't control.

"It's surface level."

He holds my gaze longer than feels necessary, and his lips are so close I wonder what they would taste like. My breathing gets shallow, and I start to squirm.

"Try to hold still, sweetheart," Gina says gently.

Pans is still looking at me, and there's a glint of triumph in his eyes. His lips curl up at the edges in a small smile as if he knows exactly what's going on in my body and my mind.

"The cut's okay, but the ankle's swollen," says Gina, completely oblivious to the weird tension that's happening on this end. "You need to rest that."

"Good thing I'm not going anywhere."

Pans lips curl right up then, and his eyes crinkle. I like making him smile. He looks hot as a hard-ass but positively breathtaking wearing a grin.

"We've got bedrooms upstairs." Gina gives Pans a prod in the side to get his attention, and the weird moment between us is gone. "I'm sure Willow will be more comfortable in a proper bed."

"No." Pans's look is back to hard-ass. "Willow stays down here."

His eyes flick back to mine, and there's a fire in them. A bolt goes through me, and I suddenly realize there's another reason Pans is keeping me locked up. He may say it's for my protection, but the sadistic hottie likes me in a cage.

Gina sighs heavily. "At least keep the door unlocked," she says.

Pans looks away, but I notice he doesn't agree to anything.

"Can you get me some more ice?" she asks Pans.

She doesn't say anything as his heavy feet tread up the stairs, but once he's gone through the door, she takes my hand and her soft eyes focus on mine.

"I want you to know that you're safe here," she says. "The Underground Crows have given you their protection, and they won't let anything bad happen to you. It's a good club, despite what you might think." She gestures at my surroundings, "The men have heart and honor, and they would never ever hurt a woman."

I want to believe her; I really do. She seems so sincere.

"Then why am I in a cage?"

Gina gives a sympathetic snort. "Because you had the

misfortune of it being Pans who rescued you and not one of the decent men."

I lie back and process what she said. There's a darkness in Pans, I feel it. And yet I feel completely safe with him.

He wants to protect me. I believe that, but locking me in a cage is completely excessive. Despite what Gina says, I don't know him or the MC.

My fingers go to the nail scissors tucked into the side of my panties. I'm indignant that I'm locked up, but something else is bubbling inside of me.

There's a part of me that finds it thrilling to be locked up in a cage. A part of me that doesn't mind being Pans's captive.

6

PANS

Gina's disapproval is obvious. I can tell by the way she looks at me as I shuffle her out the door.

"There's no need to keep her locked up, Pans."

I feel a pang of guilt. She's right. There are three bedrooms upstairs. I could make Willow comfortable. She could look out the window and hear the sound of the ocean.

She could come and go as she recovers, and there's the rub. She could leave. She could leave me.

I'm fooling myself if I believe I'm only doing this for her protection. It's because I want to keep her. I know it's not right, but the beast in me doesn't know how to keep her any other way.

And if I'm honest with myself, there's something sexy about having Willow in my cage. Knowing she's there in the basement locked up, waiting for me. I know that's all kinds of wrong, but I've never been a man who shied away from wrong.

As soon as Gina leaves, I head back down to the basement, not wanting to miss a moment with Willow. She's sitting up, the color slowly coming back to her cheeks.

"Take it easy," I tell her.

"I'm stiff," she says, stretching her arms in the air. Her tits press against her t-shirt, and I'm grateful she hasn't changed into the clothes Gina brought for her yet. I like her in my t-shirt. It marks her as mine.

"I need to move around. Can you help?"

She swings her legs over the side of the bench, and I move quickly to her side.

"Lean on me," I tell her.

She leans into my shoulder, and her weight presses against me as she stands up. My arm slides around her waist and I'm reminded of when I put her onto my bike, her soft body pressed against mine.

I stifle a groan. Just contact with this woman makes my dick ache and my chest burn. She takes a tentative step, but she's not relaxed. Her body's rigid with tension.

She reaches for something under the t-shirt, and suddenly she's lunging at me, grunting with effort as she thrusts scissors at my throat.

They're the nail scissors I used for the bandages and I don't know what damage she thinks she can do with those, but she looks determined.

I dodge backwards and grab her hand.

With her other hand she grabs at my shoulder,

37

digging her nails into me and sending us both off balance.

As we tumble to the floor, I roll over so my body lands on the hard concrete, shielding her fall as she lands on top of me. But she's wiggling too much, and I can't hold her still.

Rolling her over, I pin her to the ground. Her chest rises and falls against mine, her eyes wild and her body trembling.

"What did you do that for?" I'm bemused more than anything. Wondering why she'd try to start an attack she obviously can't win. "I'm much stronger than you."

"Why are you keeping me locked up?" Her eyes flash with a fire that does nothing to calm the growing need I have for her.

She's breathing hard, and I can smell the strawberry lip balm that Gina dropped off in her care package.

"It's for your own protection." I grit the words out through clenched teeth. She can't know the truth: that I'm scared she'll leave. That I like knowing she's down here behind bars.

Our bodies press too close, her hips wriggling against mine. I feel myself hardening, and she must feel it too because her eyes widen. But instead of disgust, there's desire in her eyes that matches my own.

My gaze flicks to her lips, parted slightly, slick with gloss. So soft and inviting. The beast inside me stirs. He uncoils, sending heat through my veins until I feel the thumping of my heart pounding in my ears.

Willow stills under me as if sensing my thoughts.

The beast rises inside, and I press my mouth against hers. She tastes of strawberries and innocence and I'm forcing this kiss in a way that I know is wrong, but I'm unable to stop. It takes me a moment to realize she's not resisting.

Her mouth parts and the forced kiss turns into a passionate back and forth, her body rising to meet mine as our tongues tangle.

My mouth moves to her neck, my teeth biting her soft flesh and making her yelp. She moves beneath me, and now she's not struggling. Her hips press against my body, her back arching until her tits graze my chest.

The beast inside urges me to part her legs, to claim what I want from this woman. I run a hand up her thigh, and she gasps as I reach her panties. My fingers nudge her thighs apart and the fabric's damp, dripping wet, the pussy beneath primed and ready to take my cock.

Alarm bells ring in the back of my mind.

She's under my protection. She's vulnerable from the accident. This isn't right. This isn't the way to take a woman, locked up in a cage and holding her down.

She's probably only yielding so that I don't hurt her. After all, what would a woman like Willow want with a beast like me?

With all the effort I can muster, I pull back onto my knees. A look of disappointment flickers across her face and then she scrambles backwards out of my reach, confirming my fears. Willow's repulsed by me, and only yielded so I'd get off her sooner.

Shame floods me, and I can't bear to look at her. I'm a beast, an animal that would debase the only woman I've ever had feelings for.

"I'm sorry," I mutter as I stand up.

I can't even look at her. I can't bear to see the disgust that must be etched on her face.

She's on the ground still and I quickly retreat out of the cage, slamming it shut and driving the lock home.

"Wait," she cries. But I can't look back. I'm too ashamed.

I take the steps two at a time until I'm through the basement door, slamming it behind me. I sink to the floor with my back to the door. Willing the beast to calm down, sucking in large gulps of air, until this raging inferno inside me subsides.

7

WILLOW

$\mathcal{I}$ don't know how many hours have passed since Pans slammed the door and stomped upstairs, shutting me out as well as shutting me in. But my lips still smart from the kiss.

The fluorescent light glows dimly, illuminating the basement. It could be the middle of the night or the middle of the day. I have no idea.

I tried to sleep but my body was too awake, remembering the press of Pans's weight on top of me, his stubble grazing my cheeks and scratching my skin, his hot breath on my throat. The hungry look in his eyes and the way he devoured me for a few blissful moments.

And then the moment he pulled back, horrified at what he was doing. Not realizing it's exactly what I want him to do.

I'm drawn to the man. Despite being in a cage, despite being locked up, or maybe because of it.

There's something dark inside him that stirs something in me. Makes me long for him to press his body against mine again, to find out where that kiss would take us. My body shudders at the memory. I've never let a man touch me the way that I want him to touch me. I'm inexperienced, still a virgin, but I would give that up for Pans.

Restless, I swing my legs over the side of the bed. The pain is not as sharp as it was earlier, but it's still a struggle to get to the table for food.

I rustle the last bag of Cheetos, but it's empty. I've devoured the snacks Gina brought me. Pans took the bread and other groceries upstairs, but he hasn't come back with a sandwich.

A tremor of fear shakes my insides. What if he's not coming back?

Who would know I'm here? How long would it take to find me? How long can I survive on Cheeto crumbs and two cans of diet Cola?

But something tells me Pans won't leave me here. He will come for me. I know from the hungry look that was in his eyes. He won't be able to stay away.

I flick through the magazine that Gina left me and discard it. I've already read it cover to cover.

I should sleep. But every time I close my eyes, I feel the press of Pans's body, the scrape of his lips, his hardness straining against me.

My thighs squeeze together and my hand wanders down my body, needing to ease this ache.

The door to the basement opens, and I sit up with a start.

"Pans?"

My voice comes out with a squeak.

Ignoring the pain in my foot, I hobble to the bars. He's carrying a plate of food, and hungry though I am, my eyes go to him. He has a hard expression on his face, as if he's trying to forget what happened between us.

"I brought you some lunch." He stops by the door of the cage and eyes me warily. "If I open the door, will you try to escape?"

I tighten my grip on the bars and give him what I hope is a defiant look.

"If you open the door, will you try to kiss me again?"

His body goes rigid, and his gaze meets mine. The heat in that look could scorch the earth.

He steps close so there's only metal bars between us.

"You can be sure, Willow, that I won't kiss you again."

Disappointment floods me, and I look down so he doesn't see my face flush with heat. I want him to kiss me. I desperately want him to kiss me. But it's obvious it was a mistake that he's not willing to repeat.

I step aside and he opens the door, putting the tray down on the table. I try not to fall on the food, but I'm so hungry I can't help myself. It's a ham sandwich with fresh bread, and I dive into it eagerly.

Pans's eyes travel to my swollen ankle, which looks slightly less purple today.

"How are you feeling?"

Confused, frustrated, and horny are all the things I don't say.

"Fine. I feel fine."

I've sat on the side of the bench bed to eat and Pans stands next to me, watching me devour the sandwich.

"Take a seat," I say, moving my arm expansively as if this is my home and he's a guest.

He grunts and sits next to me on the bed. He could have sat further down, but he sits right up close so that our thighs are nearly touching. I'm aware of the heat jumping between us, so hot it could melt butter.

"We're tracking The Reapers."

I swallow the last bite of sandwich, and it sticks in my suddenly dry throat.

"What will you do when you find them?"

Pan scratches his chin and looks away, not meeting my eyes, which makes me think that whatever the fate of The Reapers is, it won't be good.

"My main concern is for them to leave you alone," he says "To convince them you're not a threat. While you're staying on our premises, you're under our protection. But as soon as you leave here, we can't account for what happens to you."

There's a flicker of fear in his eyes that makes my chest constrict. Does Pans care what happens to me? The way I'm beginning to care about him?

I wonder what it would be like to be with this man. To always have a safe place and protection from the club.

"You said you don't have family. Where will you go?"

His words pull me out of my reverie.

The last few days have been surreal. I should be mad at my situation, but the truth is I've been healing and resting and it's been a nice distraction. I haven't had to think about the future. I've just had to exist.

"Where will I go?" I repeat the question slowly, thinking through the answer. Pans gives me an odd look.

"Where will you go once we make it safe for you? Where were you going when you had the accident?"

Oh, that's a good question. Because I don't really know. All my life I've been going, going, going. It was always my mom and me, on the road from one small town to the next, Mom picking up odd jobs here and there. Until I turned eighteen.

I woke up the day after my birthday to find her gone. She left a note saying that I was an adult now, and it was time for her to be on her own.

I didn't try to catch up with her. I was too mad. It took me a long time to want to track her down. And when I did, it was too late.

"I was going to visit my mother's grave."

The hard mask Pans's been wearing since he brought me the food disintegrates, and a softness comes into his eyes.

"I'm sorry."

"Don't be. I've been living on my own for the last three years. I've gotten used to it. My mother was a free spirit, and I always knew she would leave me one day.

I'm still coming to grips with the fact that she's left, left. Left this world for good, you know what I mean?"

There's the sting of tears in my eyes, and I blink them back. I've done my share of crying for my mom, and I know it's not what she'd want.

Pans sets a hand on my shoulder, and heat immediately surges through my body.

"Do you have any other family; anywhere else you can go?"

I shake my head.

"Everything I owned was in the back of that car. I was going to look for seasonal work in Southern California."

"You're going to pick fruit?" Pans sounds surprised.

"Why not?" I stick my chin out defiantly. "I did it with Mom when I was younger. I was going to go for the season. Maybe stay, maybe move on."

"Just because your mother lived a certain way doesn't mean you have to, Willow."

I turn away. I can't bear the intense look Pans gives me, as if he can see into my soul and see the emptiness there.

Because the truth is I've yearned to be a part of something for so long. I hated the way we moved around all the time, but I don't know anything else. I don't know how to stay.

"I'm sorry, Willow," he says as I swipe at a tear. God damn this man for bringing up so many emotions.

His fingers brush my cheek, wiping away the last of

my tears. His touch is warm, and I close my eyes. I lean my chin into the palm of his hand, and he cups my face.

I take his other hand, and without thinking bring it to my lips, brushing them over the scarred skin.

"Willow." It comes out choked, like a warning, and when I open my eyes there's a tortured look on his face.

I turn his hand over to the unblemished skin and press my lips to his wrist, feeling his pulse jump under my kiss.

"You don't know what you're unleashing," he says.

His grip tightens on my chin, and it sends a shiver all the way down my spine. My lady parts thrum as he caresses my throat.

"There's something inside me, something dark." His fingers dig into the soft skin of my throat. "I cannot unleash that on you."

His words are tight with restraint, and knowing how much he's fighting it turns me on all the more.

I clench my thighs together, wondering if he knows the affect he's having on me. Heat surges inside me as his thumb scrapes over my throat. I part my lips, waiting for the kiss.

When it comes, it's like a bolt of electricity shooting between us. My veins come alive. My blood is on fire. I feel the energy of this man, the darkness inside him fighting to get out. And I want it. I want to feel its power.

His hands slide down my neck and his fingers close around my throat; his grip tightens, and I gasp in his mouth as new sensations course through my body.

The gasp startles him, and Pans drops his hold on me and springs off the bed.

"Christ…" Pans looks pained as he runs his hands though his hair. A groan wrenches from his chest, and he staggers to the door of the cage.

"Don't leave." I try to pull him back, but with my bad leg but I'm too slow.

He slams the door behind him and locks it in place as I drag myself to the side of the cage. I don't know if he's locking me in or locking himself out.

"Pans," I call out again, and he must hear the desperation in my voice because he turns to face me.

His face is a picture of agony. The struggle that's going on inside of him is clear on his face.

"Willow, when I'm around you something comes over me." He paces as he talks, and I grip the sides of the bars and lean my heated forehead against the cool metal.

"There's a beast inside me, a darkness, and when I'm around you, I can't control it."

"Maybe I don't want you to control it." My voice comes out as a whisper, but it stops him in his tracks. "Maybe I want to see what's inside of you. Maybe I want to know all of you."

He takes a step towards me, and his fingers close over mine.

"You couldn't handle me, precious. I would break you."

"Maybe I want to be broken."

We take in deep, ragged breaths, staring at each other. His face is agonized and vulnerable, like a man broken.

"Where does it come from?" I ask suddenly. Because I see a broken man, a man battling with his demons.

I slide my hand free from his and reach through the bars to caress his face. Some of the agony relaxes from his expression.

"Talk to me, Pans. Tell me what you're so afraid of."

He stares at me for a long time, and I met his gaze, unwavering. Whatever he's got to tell me, I'm ready to hear.

After a long moment, he closes his eyes and starts to speak.

"I was in the military for a lot of years." He says it with a long exhale of breath as if that's the explanation, and maybe it is. "I was in Afghanistan."

He's still got his eyes closed, and his forehead creases as if he's reliving the memories.

"I saw too many things. I did terrible things. Things that were sanctioned because we were at war."

His eyes flick open, and they're troubled.

"I'm too broken, Willow, and too damaged. I saw the worst of humanity. I tried to be the best, but I saw the worst and I gave in to it. I made this darkness inside of me through the choices I made."

My fingers reach the furrow of his brow, wanting to smooth away his darkness. I feel for this man, what he gave up for our country.

49

"It swallowed me whole. The person that I was has become too damaged. There's no good left inside of me."

I think of Pans saving me on his bike, gently tending to my wounds.

"That's not true. You saved me. You protected me, and you could have left me to die on the road."

My hands travel down his throat, past his pulse, beating against my fingertips, down to his chest until I get to his solid heart. I press my palm to his chest.

"There's still good in here, Pans. I know there is."

Because I believe it's true. There's kindness in this man. I've experienced it.

"Whatever the military made you, it's not all of who you are."

My fingers keep moving over his chest. I lift up his T shirt and trace the scars on his body.

"Are these from Afghanistan?"

He nods quietly. I want to ask what happened, but I don't want him to relive it. Maybe one day he'll tell me. But for now, I trace the puckered skin.

"I believe in the good inside of you, Pans. I believe in you."

My ankle's been throbbing and now I sink to my knees, relieving the pain.

My lips close over the puckered skin on Pans's body, and he sucks in a sharp breath.

His hands reach for mine, stopping them.

"What are you doing?"

I look up, meeting his gaze levelly.

"I believe you're a good man. You've had some shitty experiences, and now I want to give you a little tenderness."

My lips dip to the hollow of skin above his jeans. Slowly, he releases my hands and I slide them down, between the bars to his belt buckle.

8
PANS

Willow's breath on my skin is like a scorching wind burning up my body. I feel it coursing through my blood, heating my veins and uncoiling the beast within. She doesn't know that she's playing with fire. I should stop her, but when I look down at her wide eyes and pouty lips, I don't want to

I used to be a decent man. I was a naive boy once who signed up for the military thinking he could save lives and make a difference. If there's any part of that young man left in me, he's buried too deep.

I should stop her. She's a virgin, for all I know. She's innocent. A decent man would stop her, but I'm no longer a decent man.

There'll be no going back from this with Willow.

I don't want to go back, my heart whispers.

I want this. My very soul wants this as much as the dark beast inside of me does.

So I watch and do nothing as she unbuckles my belt. I watch as her hands slide my jeans down and then my boxers. I watch as her hand runs up my thighs, making the hair stand on end with the heat.

I grab hold of the bars, because I'm a sick, twisted individual and the fact that we're separated by bars turns me on even more.

Willow's lips press gently against the end of my cock, and that jolts me back to reality. I take a step back; I can't let her do this. But Willow grabs me firmly, her hands on top of mine making my fingers dig into the cool metal.

"Stay," she pleads, and the need in her eyes is almost too much.

"You have no idea what you're unleashing. If I claim you, if I claim your mouth, then you are mine. Do you understand?"

"I want to be yours, Pans." Her fingertips brush my balls, and a nail scrapes along my skin.

God help me. My hips press toward her, my aching cock prodding through the bars of the cage. I'm thick with need, a vein throbbing as my cock aches for her lips.

She purses those beautiful pouty lips together and presses them to the end of my cock. The gentle kiss sets my nerves on edge. I'm ready to squirt my load, and all she's done is press her mouth to my tip.

That gentleness is my undoing. The way she kisses my cock with a tenderness that I've never experienced makes my chest ache even as my cock slaps against her chin, wanting more.

Her lips wrap around my shaft, and her tongue snakes out. It's clumsy and messy and like nothing I've experienced.

"Is this your first time, precious?" She pops my cock out of her mouth, and I feel the loss of her.

"I'm a virgin, Pans. I've never had a man in any way."

"You've never had a cock in your mouth?"

The thought sends a new wave of heat through me. She's innocent and the beast in me wants to destroy her, but the man wants to look after her.

"No, you're my first."

Her hot breath on my penis makes me shudder. I almost release right then. Knowing no other man has done this with her makes my balls pull up tight.

I'll be her first, her first everything.

I reach through the bars, wanting to touch her, but she pulls back. A teasing look comes into her eyes.

"You're the one who locked me up, Pans."

She won't let me touch her, and it's exquisite torture.

Her hand moves to my buttocks, gripping my ass as the other hand grips my shaft. Her hand slides down my cock, tentative at first and then moving in bolder strokes.

Her technique is clumsy. Teeth get in the way and her nails scratch. But that only adds to the sensation, contrasting with the softness of her tongue.

I grit my teeth, trying not to release too soon. I want to enjoy this first time with her virgin mouth. So plump, but ready for me. I try to leave the control with her, but the beast inside just wants to fuck her mouth hard.

Grabbing her hair, I don't let her get away this time. She released the beast, and now she must pay the price.

Willow gives a yelp and her eyes widen, but she doesn't stop.

I pull her head towards me, forcing my cock deeper into her mouth. Her shoulder slams into the metal bar, and she cries out.

I release her immediately, needing to make sure she's okay. But the look she gives me is all hunger as she sucks hard.

My hand tangles in her hair, and I pull her down my shaft. Willow gags once, her eyes going wide in surprise. Then she opens her throat, taking all of me down.

"Good girl." It comes out between gritted teeth.

Her eyes light up at the praise, and seeing how much she's enjoying it adds to my pleasure.

"You like sucking my cock?"

She moans, the sound sending vibrations over my sensitive cock as her head bobs an affirmative.

"Touch yourself, like a good girl."

Her hand runs over her chest, stopping to fondle a nipple. Then she continues down, spreading her legs, her fingers running over the damp patch of her panties.

Willow slides a hand into her panties and groans, the sound sending vibrations up my shaft. Her eyes roll into the back of her head, and knowing she's getting off on this is too much to bear.

Fisting her hair, I pull her hard toward me. Her cheek hits the bars but she looks at me with desire, and in that look, I know she's okay. My Willow can handle it rough. Which is good because I'm going to fuck her mouth senseless, and then go in there and fuck her pussy and make her mine.

My cock thrusts in and out of her wet mouth. It's messy and noisy and hard, and the pressure in my balls is building like a dam about to explode.

She groans as her fingers move over her pussy. We get a good rhythm going, slurping and sucking and thrusting, burying my dick in her mouth.

"Take all of me," I grit out as I slam into her. "Take all of me like a good girl."

Every time I pull her toward me, her cheek hits the metal. My hips grind against the bars and her cheek's plastered against them; she'll have a red mark there tomorrow, but my girl keeps on going.

Willow may be a virgin, but my god she's enjoying this mouth-fucking like a good little whore. I don't think I can take much more, but I need to see her come before I do.

"Come for me," I choke out, "Come like a good girl."

It's like she's been waiting for me to give her permission.

Her brow furrows and then she's screaming against my cock, her body tensing and her lips locking together in a deep pull.

It's too much.

I explode, shooting hot cum down her throat in thick

ropes. My darkness pouring out of me and straight down her throat.

I hold her head in place, keeping her close until every last drop, everything I am and everything I have for her, is spent.

She's taken my darkness and I feel lighter. I feel whole.

When my cock stops twitching, I release my hold on Willow's hair. She sits back, balanced unevenly on her good leg.

Her face is flushed, and I can tell by the way she's looking at me that she wants more. And that's what I'll give her. To make this woman mine properly.

Her mouth glistens, and a fleck of cum sits on her lips. Her tongue snakes out and licks it off.

"Did I do okay?"

"Honey, you were amazing."

She tries to get up, and a wince of pain crosses her face.

I'm a selfish bastard. The woman's got a sprained ankle, and I let her go down on her knees. But I also know I would do it again.

Unlocking the cage, I take Willow by the arms and help her to her feet. I notice how tired she is and curse myself for being so selfish. My arms go around her and I pull her close to me, kissing the top of her hair.

"I'm sorry, precious. Was I too rough?"

She looks up at me, and her eyes are sparkling. "I think I like it rough."

The words make me shudder. I'm naked from the waist down, and my dick twitches as it presses against her soft, thick flesh.

I'm thinking about all the ways I'm going to fuck her when my phone rings.

I'd love to ignore it but it's Bruno, and I can't ignore club business.

"Yeah?"

"We've got The Reapers. You need to come now."

It's the news I've been waiting for. The news that will make sure Willow is safe, make it safe for her to go out.

Willow's settled on the bed, and I suddenly realize how tired she is.

"Get some sleep."

Her eyes flicker open. "Aren't you staying?"

"I'd love to, but they've got the guys from the crash."

Realization dawns on her face. "Does that mean I'm safe?"

I'm happy she's safe, but it means she no longer needs my protection. I no longer have a reason to keep her here.

"Yes, Willow. You're safe. No one can hurt you now."

Her relieved smile warms my heart, and at the same time I feel my chest tighten.

I pull her blanket up and tuck her in. She's already sleeping soundly as I leave the cage. This time I leave the door wide open.

9

WILLOW

My sleep is long and dreamless. I don't know how long I'm out, but when I wake, I feel rested in a way that I haven't felt since the accident. My body feels lighter, and a warmth glows in my chest. There are new aches in my body, ones that make me blush to remember.

A smile pulls at my lips as I think about what happened with Pans. I don't know what came over me. I've never been so bold with a man, but I wanted to connect with him and show him tenderness.

I didn't know he was going to be so rough. The way he grabbed my hair, the way he pulled my head down his shaft--just thinking about it sends a delicious wave of heat between my legs.

Pans was rough, and I liked it.

I sit up on the bench bed, and the first thing I notice is

that the door to the cage is wide open. For the first time, I'm not locked in.

I should feel relieved. But strangely, I feel desolate. It's silent, no creaking from upstairs, and with the door hanging open, it feels like I've been abandoned.

"Pans!" I call out, but there's no answer.

I swing my legs over the side of the bed and carefully lower myself to the floor. My ankle still throbs, but it's not nearly as bad as it was.

Holding the metal bars for support, I hobble out of my cage. There's a railing on the side of the staircase, and I use that to help me up the stairs. I'm sweating by the time I get to the top of them. But the door opens.

"Pans?" I call. But the house is silent.

An uneasy feeling gnaws at the pit of my stomach. He wouldn't have abandoned me, would he? He must still be on club business.

It takes me a good few minutes to explore the cottage, hobbling between rooms and stopping to catch my breath. In the few days I've been resting, my body has gotten weak.

In the main living room, there's an empty beer can on the coffee table and a stack of car magazines, but no signs of life.

In the kitchen, I find the bread and make myself a cheese sandwich, gulping it down hungrily and washing it down with a glass of water.

There's a large bedroom at the end of the hall, and the window looks out over a valley of dense trees and all the way to the ocean. There's a duffle bag in the corner and the bedsheets are ruffled. I guess this is where Pans has been sleeping.

When I open the window, I can make out the distant sound of waves crashing.

I breathe deep, filing my lungs with salty air. And then it hits me. I'm free.

Pans said they caught the man who was after me. I don't know what they'll do to him. But I trust that Pans will make sure it's safe for me.

I'm finally free.

Pans has been nothing but kind to me, keeping me safe in his weird way. But I'm sure I'm nothing but a plaything for him. What would an older man want with a tubby younger girl like me?

But now that I'm free, there's nothing stopping me from walking out the door.

I could walk right out of here or hobble out of here. I could catch a ride and continue on my way to mom's grave and the fruit farms of Southern California.

Gina brought my purse to me which had my phone and wallet. I don't need my other possessions.

I could go before Pans gets back and realizes his mistake. If he's even coming back for me.

What if he got what he wanted and now he's set me free? Maybe that's why he left the cage open.

A cold shiver goes down my spine. I rushed into things with a man I barely know. How did I expect it to end?

All my life, I watched my mother pack up and leave as soon as the going got tough. One failed relationship after another.

Her words ring in my ears.

"It's always better to be the one that leaves than the one that gets left behind."

I was sure there was a connection with Pans, but what do I know about men?

I try the front door, and it's unlocked.

As soon as I open it, the cool breeze hits me. Insects call in the trees and I close my eyes, loving the feel of the breeze on my face after having been locked away.

I felt a connection with Pans, but is it worth sticking around for?

My heart beats heavy as I head to the basement. Grabbing the bag that Gina left, I stuff it with my few belongings and the last can of soda.

I whisper a goodbye to the cage and drag my bag up upstairs.

10

PANS

The lines of the road blur underneath my bike as I speed up the highway. I can't get away from the clubhouse fast enough. My need to get back to Willow is so strong I ride like a man possessed.

We questioned the men from The Reapers. There was a price to pay for bringing drugs into our territory, and they paid it in blood.

Before Willow I probably wouldn't have let them live, but she sees something better in me. She makes me want to be better.

So I left them bloody but alive, and with an understanding that there's no going after the witness. That she's under our club's protection permanently.

She will be once I give her my cut. Then everyone will know Willow is my property. You mess with her, you mess with me, and the whole club will fight in her corner.

Fear grips me as I wind down the road to the cottage. I left the cage unlocked, but now I wonder if that was the right thing to do. What if she's gone?

I bring the bike to a screeching stop, kicking up gravel as I cut the engine.

"Willow!" I call as I fling open the front door.

I take the stairs to the basement two at a time, gripping my stomach. I need to see her; I need to see her face.

The cage is empty.

My breath catches, and a low groan wells up in my chest and surfaces through my throat.

Of course she's gone. I left her cage unlocked. I set her free. Why would she stick around for a beast like me?

I was sure we had a connection. But maybe that was just my mind playing tricks. Maybe it was what I wanted to feel.

I go into the cage, tearing it apart as if she might be hidden under the bench. But it's empty, and her purse is gone.

I head up the stairs calling her name. Frantically racing through the cottage and checking all the rooms.

She's not in the kitchen, she's not in the lounge, and she's not in the bedrooms. I left the cage open, and the bird has flown.

Throwing open the front door, I cry her name into the trees, an agonized shout that sends a flock of birds cawing into the sky.

But all I hear back is the hum of cicadas.

I slump onto the stoop with my head in my hands.

If you love something, you're supposed to set it free. But no one ever tells you about the pain that comes when it takes that freedom.

I should have listened to the beast inside. I should have kept her caged up.

But I know I did the right thing; I did the decent thing. And now she's gone.

I could follow her, but what would I do if I found her? Lock her up again? As much as I want to, I can't keep her caged up forever.

I have to accept that my precious Willow is gone.

Footsteps on the gravel make my head jerk up.

Willow stands in front of me like a vision from the angels. She's holding a bowl, and her lips are stained dark purple.

"I went to pick blackberries," she says breezily. "I noticed the bushes around here. I thought I'd make us a pie."

I'm too stunned to answer, and she steps past me and into the house.

My hand slides after her and grabs her good ankle. She stops, startled.

"You stayed."

My voice is full of wonder, and I'm still trying to process it. She gives me a smile, and I feel my heart crack.

I let her free, and she came back. She came back. That means she's mine.

"I thought you had gone. Your bags…" I trail off.

"I moved them to your bedroom," she says shyly. "I

hope you don't mind. It's a lot more comfortable up there. And you can see the ocean from the window."

I pull myself up and take her in my arms.

"I thought I'd scared you off."

My hands grip her arms, needing to know she's really here.

"It'll take a lot more than that to scare me off. I'm not afraid of your darkness, Pans. And I know the decent man will win when he needs to."

Her words reverberate around my body. All these years I thought the beast inside me, uncontrollable and dark, made me unfit for human company. And with one sentence this woman has put the beast in its place.

"Willow, you have no idea what you do to me. You unleash the beast in me and also tame it. I thought I was broken and no one could love me. You've shown me what love can do. I'll always love you, Willow."

Hips brush up against mine, sending an immediate jolt to my body.

I pull her against me so hard and sudden that the bowl of berries goes crashing to the ground. But I don't care. My lips devour hers as I push her against the wall, squishing berry juice into the carpet.

My hand moves down her throat, feeling the rapid beat of her pulse. The darkness rises inside me, and I pull back. If I truly want to be a better man, I should go gently, give her the tenderness she deserves.

"What are you doing?" Willow whines.

"Your first time should be tender."

"Can you do tender?"

"I don't know, but I want to try."

Her brow furrows. "But I don't want that. I want the beast, Pans. I want your darkness."

Her eyes are hooded and her breathing heavy.

"Are you sure?"

She bites her bottom lip and nods. "I think I like it rough."

Could this woman be any more perfect?

I hoist her up by the hips, and she wraps her legs around me as I carry her to the bedroom.

11

WILLOW

*P*ans throws me on the bed, and I give a little bounce before his body crashes into mine. If this is being gentle, I wonder what rough sex would be like

His hand scrapes my hair back, cupping my face.

"Willow, I love you."

A warmth fills my heart. It's been less than a week since I met this man, but I'm so certain of him, so sure that our lives are meant to be entwined.

I've always been a gentle soul. That's what my mom always said, and maybe this is what I'm meant to do. Heal this man, coax out the gentleness that I know is inside him.

But right now, it's the animal inside, the beast as he calls it, that I want to see.

Pans tugs off my panties, and I shiver as the cool air

hits my pussy. Then his mouth closes over me, and warm breath blows over my most sensitive bits.

The new sensations wash over me as his tongue flicks against my hard core. My back arches and I grab the sheets, the sensation almost too much to bear.

Pans is everything I thought he would be, rough and unpredictable with his tongue, plunging it into my pussy then licking my hard nub. Driving me wild with never knowing what's coming next.

Just when I think I can't bear it anymore, he slows down. His roving tongue gently laps at my clit, and his fingers brush against my sticky entrance.

I practically purr at his soft touch; at the sensitive side he's showing me. I sigh at the slow way he moves his mouth, kissing my pussy lips. When his finger slides inside, I cry out in surprise. I've never had anything inside me before, and the new sensation makes me hungry for more.

As if reading my mind, Pans slips another finger into me and then a finger into my back passage.

I sit up on the bed, not sure how I feel about this new intrusion. Pans looks up, his chin glistening with pussy juice, and gives me a wicked look.

"Relax, Willow," he says. "Now you're mine. I have to claim every part of you."

His finger moves inside me, and I groan at the sensation. He thrusts his hand deeper, his intense gaze on mine.

"You're mine forever, Willow. You'll always have my protection."

Warmth surges through me as he dips his head and gets back to my aching pussy. His pace quickens and I meet every finger thrust with my hips, wanting more, wanting it deeper in both entrances.

Pans talks about his beast, but he's unleashed something inside of me too. Grabbing the back of his head, I pull his face onto my pussy, sliding up and down against his face as my climax builds. I feel wanton, I feel dirty, and I feel completely safe.

Then I don't feel anything but pleasure. Waves and waves of it coursing through my body as I fall over the cliff of my climax, my openings clenching against his palm, squeezing his fingers so hard I think they might get stuck inside me.

But Pans doesn't stop. Relentlessly, he works my pussy through the orgasm until it tumbles into the next one, and I'm screaming his name as I grip his face to my pussy, my legs sticking straight up in the air.

Only when I stop shaking does he come up for air. But only for a moment.

He's grinning as he shimmies up the bed and kisses me hard. I taste my own tangy flavor on his lips.

Fumbling with his belt, I tug his clothes off. The two orgasms have only made my pussy more needy for him, hungry to feel him inside me.

Pans kneels over me, his cock sticking straight out, a bead of pre-cum hanging from the tip.

My pussy clenches in anticipation. Wanting to feel him inside me, I push my hips forward.

"Claim me, Pans. Make me yours."

He grips the base of his cock and gives a hard stroke.

"I'll try to be gentle, precious."

"You don't need to be gentle. I want you to be rough. I want you to be yourself."

His eyes burn with desire at my words, but still he hesitates.

"You don't know what you're asking, Willow. I could break you."

"Then show me." My fingers slide down my tits. Pans's gaze follows their path as I tug on my already hard nipples.

Suddenly, his hands are on my hips and he flips me over on the bed, my face hitting the duvet.

I give a gasp of surprise as his fingers dig into my hips, pulling my ass into the air.

A surge of wet heat pools in my pussy and drips slowly down my thigh as his cock presses between my ass cheeks.

"I'll let myself go if that's what you want." His breath is hot on my neck, the low base rumble making my insides melt. "But if you want me to stop, you tap the bed twice like this." He taps the mattress like a wrestler tapping out.

"And if you can't reach the bed, you tap my thigh, my shoulder, wherever you can reach. You tap out, and I'll stop immediately."

I nod. A twinge of nervousness vibrates through my body, but it only adds to the anticipation.

"But if you don't tap out…" He nips my neck, his teeth scraping my skin. "I will keep going and going and going. You understand?"

I nod.

"Say it, Willow. I need to hear your voice."

"Yes," I croak. "Can you please fuck me now?"

Pans give a low wicked laugh and runs his hand down my back. It rests on my ass before he pulls it back and slaps my butt cheek.

I yelp in surprise, but the sting only adds to my desire.

"I want this, Pans. Give me your darkness. Let me absorb it."

He sucks in a breath. There's a moment of stillness, and then he's on me, his cock prodding my entrance, pushing in and stretching my pussy.

One hand grabs my tit, pinching the nipple, and I know I'll be bruised in the morning, but right now, I don't care. All I care about is the feel of his cock as he guides the tip inside.

I swivel my hips back, wanting more and wondering what he's waiting for.

I feel sick with anticipation, dripping wet and needing a release. I'm ready for him. I'm nervous and I'm excited all at once.

All of a sudden he thrusts home, and I cry out as white heat burns my insides. I've never felt so full, and I'm so stretched I might burst.

I grab the sheet, howling into it as Pans stills, but only for a moment. Then he slides right out of me.

"I've got your virgin blood on my cock."

There's wonder in his voice and I'm so glad I gave that to him, but now that I've had a taste, I want him back inside me.

"Please," I whimper, "don't stop."

Before the words are out of my mouth, Pans thrusts into me again, going hard and deep until his balls slap against me.

"Take it like a good girl, Willow."

And I do. I take his cock and I rock my hips and I moan, wanting more and more and more of him.

Pleasure builds inside me, but I need some friction. My hand slides up my thigh, and I touch my hot spot. It's sticky and I trace slow circles, my hand reaching around so my fingernails scrape his balls.

Every time he pitches forward, I pinch his balls, and I love the way it makes him groan.

We're facing the window in the room and the light outside has faded, showing us our reflection in the glass. Pans pounds me from behind as I touch myself, our faces contorted with pleasure and urgency.

His eyes meet mine and he's like a wild animal, a lion mounting its mate. His teeth are bared as he gets more frenzied, slamming into me with no mercy.

With his eyes on mine, he leans forward. His arm slides between my breasts, and his hand closes around my throat.

"You're mine, Willow, all mine," he grunts out as his fingers tighten on my skin. It should be terrifying, but it heightens the sensations claiming my body.

I keep eye contact as he pounds me like a rag doll, pulling me onto his cock time and time again.

My vision blurs and my pussy clenches and then I'm falling over the edge, my body convulsing in ecstasy, the orgasm so intense that I think I might pass out.

Pans gives a final thrust and then explodes inside of me, yelling out my name. He sits back and pulls me onto his thighs, making sure I capture every last drop of his cum.

Our eyes meet in the reflection of the window. We're both panting, and there are red marks around my throat. Pans's eyes go to them, and his expression changes.

"Willow, I didn't mean to hurt you. Why didn't you tap out?"

I run my hands over my throat and the raw marks that prove I belong to Pans. There's no mistaking he owns me, and God helped me I liked it. I liked it so much.

"Because I didn't want you to stop."

Pans turns me toward him, and we lay together on the bed. His fingers caress my neck, gentle now and soft.

I'm overwhelmed by the contrast, the rough lover and the gentle man.

"I can swallow your darkness, Pans; I can take it. But you know there are people who can help," I say. "Have you ever done that?"

He shakes his head. "I don't think there's help for people like me."

I let it drop, but I know there's a way to help my troubled man. And maybe being by his side is all I need to do. And together maybe we'll heal.

"I love you, Pans."

"I love you too, precious. I will always have this darkness inside of me. But with you by my side, it won't overwhelm me."

He kisses me gently and I lean into him, already feeling sleepy.

"My name is Simon." It croaks out of his mouth, rusty from being unused.

"Simon," I repeat. And then again more forcefully. "I love you, Simon."

Simon smiles and I close my eyes, safe and happy in his embrace.

EPILOGUE

WILLOW

Two years later…

I shift the weight of the baby from my left hip to the right side. He squirms in my arms and reaches for the bowl of salad that I'm juggling in my other hand.

"Uh-uh, not for you," I say gently and he pouts at me, making me laugh.

"You'll get yours in a minute, don't you worry little guy."

Using my butt to push the door open, I take the salad from the kitchen into the main room of the clubhouse.

Gina frowns at me as she takes the bowl from my hands.

"Go sit down, Willow. We'll take it from here."

"Are you sure? There're still the potatoes to finish off."

She gives a pointed look at my round belly and the one-year-old tugging on my hair.

"You should be resting."

I don't need to be told twice. Not that there's any rest with a baby who crawls faster than I can walk.

I've been busy in the kitchen all day helping the other women prepare the food. It was easy when Dale was sleeping, but now he's awake and tugging at my T shirt looking for something to eat.

Gina gives me a warm smile. "Go feed your baby and put your feet up."

The tables have been pushed together so they're ready for the club dinner. The smell of barbecue wafts in from outside, and the whole place has a festive feel to it.

I love these club dinners, the whole family getting together, because that's what the club has become to me. A family.

I drag over my diaper bag and take a seat. It's too tricky balancing Dale on my lap with him wiggling so much, so I set him on the ground while I pull out plastic tubs of baby food.

He's off across the floor before I can stop him, making a beeline for Lily. He stops in front of her, tugging on her skirt until she notices him.

"Hello, Dale." She scoops him into her arms, and he beams with pleasure. I can't blame him. With Lily's long flowing hair and bright green eyes, she's a real beauty.

Jesse watches them from his table in the corner, a wistful look in his eyes, and I can't help but think Dale's not the only one who has a crush on the President's daughter.

Lily brings Dale back to me, making him giggle as she bounces him on her hip. She nods at the tubs of baby food.

"You want me to heat that up for you?"

I give her a grateful smile. "Thank you."

She hands Dale back to me, who gives a regretful sigh.

"Just 30 seconds in the microwave," I call after her.

"I know," she says over her shoulder.

If the saying is true that it takes a village to raise a child, then the clubhouse is my village. There's always someone here to mind the kids if needed. The Pres installed a swing-set out back when he had his first kid, and now there are always kids around.

Dale's not just being raised by me and Pans. All the women here and the men too are looking out for him.

I feel Pans's presence before I see him. The air in the clubhouse goes thick and I turn around to find his gaze on me, leaning on the back door and watching me with his son.

He walks in with some of the men. I don't ask questions about where they've been or what they've done. I've learned not to ask about club business.

Pans comes straight to me. And I see by the set lines of his face that it's something I don't want to know about.

I set Dale on the floor as Pans kneels in front of us.

His mouth presses to mine and I run my hands over

78

his face, the bristly stubble so familiar to me now. I cup his cheeks in my hands and hold him there for a few minutes, letting him breathe in and out, releasing whatever's troubling him.

By the time he looks up, he's grinning.

"How's my little man?"

He chucks his son under his chin and scoops him up off the floor. Dale squeals in delight, happy to be held by his father.

My heart warms for the man who gave me a family. Pans may not have exorcised all his demons, but I know he's a calmer man than when I first met him.

Pans refused counseling, so we do our own brand of healing. In the bedroom, his beast comes out and I absorb his pain, craving his dark energy as much as he does. Needing to feel him release into me. Afterwards, we're both centered and connected. He's loving and affectionate in a way I never thought he could be.

We got married in a rush when we found out I was pregnant. Six months after Dale arrived, we found out I was pregnant again.

And who knows when it will stop. I love my baby, and I love this life.

Lily comes back with the baby food, and Pans sits Dale on his knee to feed him. I tell him about my day, and he tells me what he can of his.

Lily passes us again on her way to the kitchen, and I notice Jesse's eyes following her.

She's the Pres's daughter, and by that right she's out of

bounds to all the men. But I've seen the way that Jesse always finds excuses to be near her.

A moment later he gets up and follows her into the kitchen. When he comes back, they're both carrying plates of food and she's laughing at something he said.

I smile to myself, wondering...

I spend a lot of time sitting and feeding and it gives me time to observe the club members. They're a good bunch of men and woman. They can be tough to outsiders, but they follow their own moral code.

I feel protected here. I always have, especially with Pans next to me. I know without a doubt what he would do to anyone who hurt me.

Dale smiles, and I break into a grin. I look up at Pans and he's grinning right back at me, both of us wrapped up in the love we have for our child. It suits my man, a smile on his face. I feel a surge of love go out to him as we share the look of proud parents.

Being a parent can be exhausting. But with Pans and the club by my side. I wouldn't have it any other way.

The food's brought to the table, and everyone takes a seat. There's clinking of plates and chatter as we sit down as a family to eat.

This is my family, the family I've chosen or the family that chose me. I've never been sure which. I'm just glad I'm here.

We're halfway through the meal when the door opens abruptly. The men instantly scrape their chairs back, ready to face the intruder.

A tall man stands in the doorway, silhouetted by the burning orange light of sunset. All is silent for a minute. Then noise erupts all at once.

Bruno strides forward and slaps the man heartily on the back. Gage lets out a whoop and embraces the man like he's a long lost brother.

I look around the table bewildered, wondering what's going on. The other women look as confused as I am.

Apart from Gina. She's gone white as a sheet and her hand, poised halfway to her mouth holding a water glass, is trembling.

I look back at the stranger. He's stepped into the light now and I can see he's rugged and handsome, with a thick beard and sharp, intelligent eyes.

His gaze sweeps the room and lands on Gina. He smiles at her.

Gina gasps, and her glass smashes to the floor.

"Hi Gina." He's got a foreign brogue that may be Irish. "I'm back."

* * *

WHAT TO READ NEXT

MOUNTAIN MAN'S OBSESSION

His one obsession is her...

From the moment Colette sweeps into my bar, I can't stop watching her. Even when she doesn't know I'm looking. *Especially* then.

My cameras record her every smile, every frown, every moment. I study her until I know my girl inside out, my obsession growing, overwhelming me, demanding I act.

She'll never find out my secret, will she?

Mountain Man's Obsession features an OTT obsessed mountain man and the curvy innocent woman he claims as his own. It's high heat, oh so sweet, and always with a happily ever after.

Keep reading for an exclusive excerpt or visit:
mybook.to/MMObsession

MOUNTAIN MAN'S OBSESSION

CHAPTER ONE

Bear

Her fingers pause in their flight across the keyboard. She sits back, nibbling the tip of her thumb, a self-conscious gesture, unaware of me watching her.

She sits upright in the booth her chestnut hair hanging in loose waves under her headphones.

"I guess she doesn't like your choice of music," Kit, my best buddy, quips as he follows my gaze.

Dragging my eyes away from the beauty in the corner, I pull him a pint of strong ale and set it on the bar in front of him. "She's concentrating."

He takes a sip, his gaze resting on her a little longer than I'm comfortable with.

"I wonder what she's writing."

My body stiffens. I'm not happy that he's showing

interest in my girl. Well, not technically my girl yet, but she will be.

I cut a look at my best buddy but his gaze has already left her. He sips his beer and scans the room. Either he knows she's mine, or he's not interested. Hopefully the latter. I'd hate to have to fight my best friend.

"Historical romance."

He gives me a pointed look. "You've spoken to her, then?"

That's not how I know what she's writing but I'm not going to tell him my secret.

"We've met. Her name's Colette."

The name swirls around my tongue and sends a shiver of longing through my body, my blood thumping in my ears.

My Colette.

To hide my reaction, I grab a tray of glasses from the dishwasher and start drying them. Kit gets the hint and drops the subject.

While I put the glasses away, Kit leans against the bar. Suddenly he sets his beer down and his eyes narrow.

"Who's that with your sister?"

I follow his gaze, and my chest tightens.

Ursula's seated at her usual table with her best friend, Heather. I served them low alcohol vodka in their cocktails, but they don't know that.

There are two guys at the table with them. One is leaning over Ursula with a leery look on his preppy boy face.

I know everyone of drinking age in Maple Falls, population 1,300-ish, and I don't recognize these kids. They're either up from Maple Springs for the night or tourists, here for the hiking trails.

Since my parents passed in a climbing accident eight years ago, I not only inherited the bar, but responsibility for my little sister as well. It was easier when she was still at school. But now she's twenty-two and just home from college, and every randy boy on the mountain is trying to get in her pants.

Not on my watch.

Slinging my dishcloth over my shoulder, I approach her table and cross my arms, so my muscles are on display alongside my tattoos. I fix my eyes on the skinny boy staring at my sister's tits.

"Evening, gentlemen."

My voice comes out as a low growl. I'm a big guy, six-foot-five and almost as wide as the mountain.

The kid jumps when he sees me and the leery look slides off his face.

Ursula looks like she wants to stab me in the eye. "Bear. What are you doing?"

"You know this guy?" the spotty kid stammers.

"He's my brother." Ursula rolls her eyes. "Here to protect my virtue."

"Can I see your ID?"

Kit comes up behind me, as if I need back up, but he's almost as protective of my sister as I am.

The boy fumbles in his pocket and shares a look with his friend.

"We, um left it in the car. I'll just go get it."

They scamper through the door and Kit follows, watching them all the way to the car park.

"Do you think they're coming back?" Heather asks wistfully.

"No," says Ursula. "Would you come back if this guy threatened you?" She gestures at me.

"You'll thank me for it one day, sis."

"When I die a lonely old maid?" She gives me a sarcastic smile, but her eyes are dancing, and I know I'm already forgiven. My sister's too smart to go for a gangly kid like that anyway.

Kit returns and I motion him over, putting my hand on his shoulder.

"Keep these ladies company would you, Kit? Make sure those young bucks don't come sniffing around again."

"Sure." He doesn't hesitate, which is why he's my best friend. Always willing to help out, even if it means babysitting my sister.

On my way back to the bar, I do the rounds clearing tables and talking to my regulars.

The Amery brothers are in town, Chase as chatty and good natured as his brother Rowan is surly and silent. Rowan's ex-military, and I give him a drink on the house whenever he's in town. Which isn't often. Doesn't like people much, that one.

The only person I don't chat with is Ewan, the recluse who never talks. He likes to sit on his own, staring at the mountain and sipping his whiskey. I can't imagine what demons he's wrestling with inside. But it's not my place to judge, only to serve.

His glass is empty, and I bring him another whiskey. Scotch, to go with his Scottish accent. He nods at me and silently raises his glass in thanks.

By the time I get around to Colette's booth, she's gone. There's an empty coffee mug and a napkin. On the napkin is a faint imprint of her lips, shiny and coffee stained, like she's pressed them to her lip-balm covered mouth.

Glancing around the bar to check no one's watching, I press the napkin to my own lips, right on the imprint. It smells like cherry lip balm and coffee, exactly how I imagine she'll taste when I finally kiss her.

Slipping the napkin in my pocket, I take the empty mug to the bar.

Later that night, the last punters finally go home, so I lock up and go upstairs to my apartment above the bar.

With eager fingers, I open my laptop and pull up the CCTV feed from the bar. The live feed shows it's all quiet downstairs, but that's not what I'm here to look at. I scroll back until I find the recordings from earlier tonight. Until I find Colette.

There's one CCTV camera trained on the bar, another one pointing outwards toward the door, and a third pointing to the left-hand side of the bar. Then there's the one I installed last week, after the first time she walked into Bear's Brewery.

She blew in with a flurry of autumn leaves, all five-foot-nothing and wrapped up in a red coat and matching knitted hat, her hair splayed out behind her. Her cheeks were rosy red, her eyes bright, and her beauty so surprising that the glass I was holding dropped right out of my hand. It shattered on the floor along with my heart.

She smiled at me and ordered a coffee then selected the booth in the corner, the one overlooking the mountain.

While I burnt the coffee and over-frothed the milk, she pulled out her laptop and put on a set of headphones.

For the first hour, she just stared at the mountain, letting her coffee go cold. It made me agitated, watching her. I wanted to know what she was doing, where she'd come from, but she was in such a reverie I didn't want to disturb her.

Then she began to type.

The next day, she came back and repeated the ritual in the same booth.

That night, I installed my fourth CCTV camera, above the booth. That's the feed I pull up now.

I've watched her every night since. Replaying the feed, pausing and zooming in to see what she's writing, to catch her smile, to examine the lines of concentration on her face when she's thinking.

I know every expression, every turn of her mouth. I know the thumbnail on her right hand is worn down from nibbling it when she's thinking. I know she sometimes hums along to whatever music is in her headphones. I know she smiles along with her characters and mouths the words when she's writing dialogue.

There's no explanation for this obsession. I should talk to her, ask her out. But then I'd have no reason to watch her. And I like watching her.

She's so petite, but there's nothing petite about her curves. She must think I'm a brute with my height and bulk and rugged beard. Plus, she writes romance. I know this from reading her screen. What does a guy like me, raised on the mountain from a long line of mountain families, know about romance?

So, I watch, and I wait, looking for the right opportunity to show her we're meant to be together.

I scroll back to when she arrived today, pausing on her face as she stares out the window. There's a serenity to her, a peacefulness that's endearing.

Under her coat she wears a tight sweater. Her breasts are pushed against the fabric.

That's what catches my eye now – her tits straining to be let out.

I imagine them in my hand, caressing her nipples as I ravage her body.

Undoing my fly, I catch my dick in my hand. Thinking about her curvy body writhing under me, I thrust into my palm.

Remembering the napkin, I grab it from my pocket and press it against my nostrils, inhaling her scent. It's all I need to send me over the edge, shooting hot liquid into my palm.

Breathing hard, I set the napkin down alongside the other memorabilia I've collected.

One day, I'll talk to her, make her mine. But for now, I'm content to watch.

To keep reading visit:
mybook.to/MMObsession

GET YOUR FREE BOOK

Sign up to the Sadie King mailing list for a FREE book!

You'll be the first to hear about new releases, exclusive offers, bonus content and all my news. You can even email me back. I love chatting with my readers!

To claim your free book visit:
www.authorsadieking.com/free

BOOKS BY SADIE KING

Sunset Coast

Underground Crows MC

Sunset Security

Men of the Sea

The Thief's Lover

The Henchman's Obsession

The Hitman's Redemption

Maple Springs

Men of Maple Mountain

All the Single Dads

Candy's Café

Small Town Sisters

Kings County

Kings of Fire

King's Cops

For a full list of titles check out the Sadie King website

www.authorsadieking.com

ABOUT THE AUTHOR

Sadie King is a USA Today Best Selling Author of short instalove romance.

She lives in New Zealand with her ex-military husband and raucous young son.

When she's not writing she loves catching waves with her son, running along the beach, and good wine, preferably drunk with a book in hand.

Keep in touch when you sign up for her newsletter. You'll even snag yourself a free short romance!

www.authorsadieking.com/free

Ingram Content Group UK Ltd.
Milton Keynes UK
UKHW040809200723
425492UK00001B/12

9 798215 139615